Patricia's Visit

to the

Hospital

Patrice N. Rivers

inner child press, ltd.

Credits

Author

Patrice N. Rivers

Illustrator

Vineet Kumar Siddhartha

Cover Graphic & Design

Vineet Kumar Siddhartha

Editor

hülya n. yılmaz, Ph.D.

General Information

Patricia's Visit to the Hospital
Patrice N. Rivers

1st Edition: 2020

Publisher Information:

Inner Child Press
intouch@innerchildpress.com
www.innerchildpress.com

This Collection is protected under U.S. and International Copyright Laws

Copyright © 2020: Patrice N. Rivers

ISBN-13: 978-1-952081-27-9 (inner child press, ltd.)

$ 19.95

Dedication

This book is dedicated to the Sickle Cell Community. To all the children around the world living with Sickle Cell Disease, keep your head up and remember that you are a warrior!

September
is
SICKLE CELL
Awareness
Month

Acknowledgements

Thanks are due to my illustrator, Vineet Siddhartha, for the wonderful illustrations as always and to my wonderful publishing company, Inner Child Press International, for the hard work and dedication.

The Author's Introduction

Sickle Cell Disease not only affects African-Americans, but other demographics in countries such as the Caribbean, Greece, Puerto Rico, India, Egypt and Canada. It's funny that a lot of people classify Sickle Cell Disease as a "Black-only' disease. Yes, it's true that mostly African-Americans are affected by it, but it's deeper than one race. My new children's book *Patricia's Visit to the Hospital* is a part of a series called *Come Learn with Patricia*, and I plan to write more children books within the series to educate and talk about the importance of Sickle Cell Disease.

I was diagnosed with SCD at the age of one. Both of my parents are carriers of the Sickle Cell Trait. I wanted to share my story through writing a children's book because many kids may not understand what is fully going on when they may be in pain or when they are hospitalized. My first book of the series, *Patricia's Guardian Angel* and the new one both come from a place of experience in my childhood while I was fighting for my life with pain crises.

I feel like SCD isn't talked about enough throughout the communities and I always showed interest trying to not only share my story but to continue to support it. What better way than to market this book and write this book that serves a greater cause than actually reading a children's book; this children's book to your children, grandchildren, nieces, nephews, cousins, etc.? It's an educational book to educate parents, children and others about what kids living with SCD really go through.

I personally suffered my most severe pain crises as a child to a point where the second pain crisis I had almost killed me in 1999 at the age of twelve. People die every day battling with Sickle Cell Disease. It's really important to become educated on it and to know more about it and why SCD should be talked about more in public schools, health fairs, churches, meetings and definitely in the communities. Just like cancer, diabetes, aids, lupus, heart disease and other diseases are talked about, SCD should be too! Don't only purchase this book and just read it, but understand it and market it and make sure you share it with other people in your community.

Patrice N. Rivers

Patricia's Visit

to the

Hospital

"Patricia, it's time to wake up! Breakfast is on the table. We have to make a move soon to the doctors", Mommy said. I slowly got up and began to frown. I was feeling sick and cold, and I could barely move out of bed.

"MOMMYYY!!!" I screamed at the top of my lungs. My mom came in my room, and I began to cry.

"What's wrong, Patricia? And why aren't you out of bed yet?"

"Mommy, I don't feel well. I feel tired and weak", I said reaching for my mom to pick me up.

Mommy felt my head and noticed that I was warm. After taking my temperature, Mommy realized that I was running a temperature of 102.

After giving me my bath and getting me dressed, Mommy then took me to the ER. I cried the whole way to the ER because I was in pain and felt yucky. When Mommy and I got to the hospital, Mommy signed in and started filling out paperwork. I looked around and saw a lot of other kids with their mommies and daddies with them.

"Mommy, is daddy coming?" I asked sadly.

"Yes, your Daddy is on his way now", she said and hugged me tightly.

A tall lady nurse came out and called us back to a small room. "Hi, Patricia. I'm Nurse Davenport and I hear that you have a fever and aren't feeling well. Are you in pain as well?" The nurse asked.

"I feel a little pain in my back. It's sharp and I don't like it", I mumbled.

"Well, let me take a look at you and listen to your breathing."

Nurse Davenport lifted me up on the table as she pulled up my shirt. I started to giggle. "That's cold", I screeched out loud.

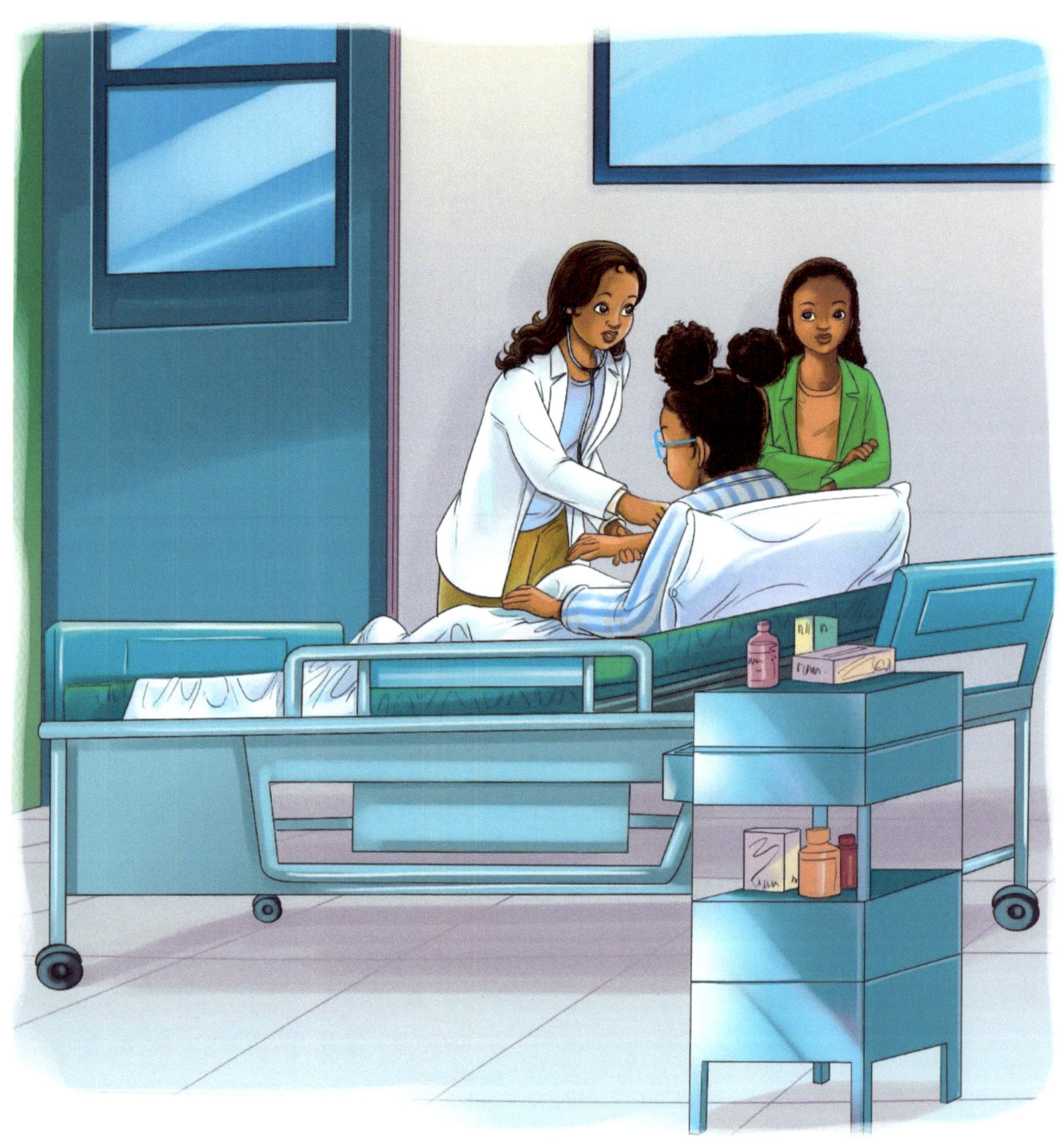

Both the nurse and Mommy laughed. After running some tests, the doctors wanted to keep me over night. Along with my fever, I was diagnosed with an acute chest syndrome. I hated the fact that I had to spend the night at the hospital. I will miss going to school and seeing my friends, especially Shaunie who is my best friend. Daddy then came in and said he was spending the night with me. I was excited because it will be just like a slumber party like at one of my birthday parties.

After I got something to eat, Doctor Bryant and the nurse said I have to drink plenty of water. I wanted some juice, but couldn't have it at the moment. Daddy brought my favorite stuffed animal from home, and we all played until the pain became more severe. This time, it was hurting more and more, and I kept tossing and turning in my bed. Nurse Davenport gave me some pain medicine to make me relax. I began to dream happy thoughts.

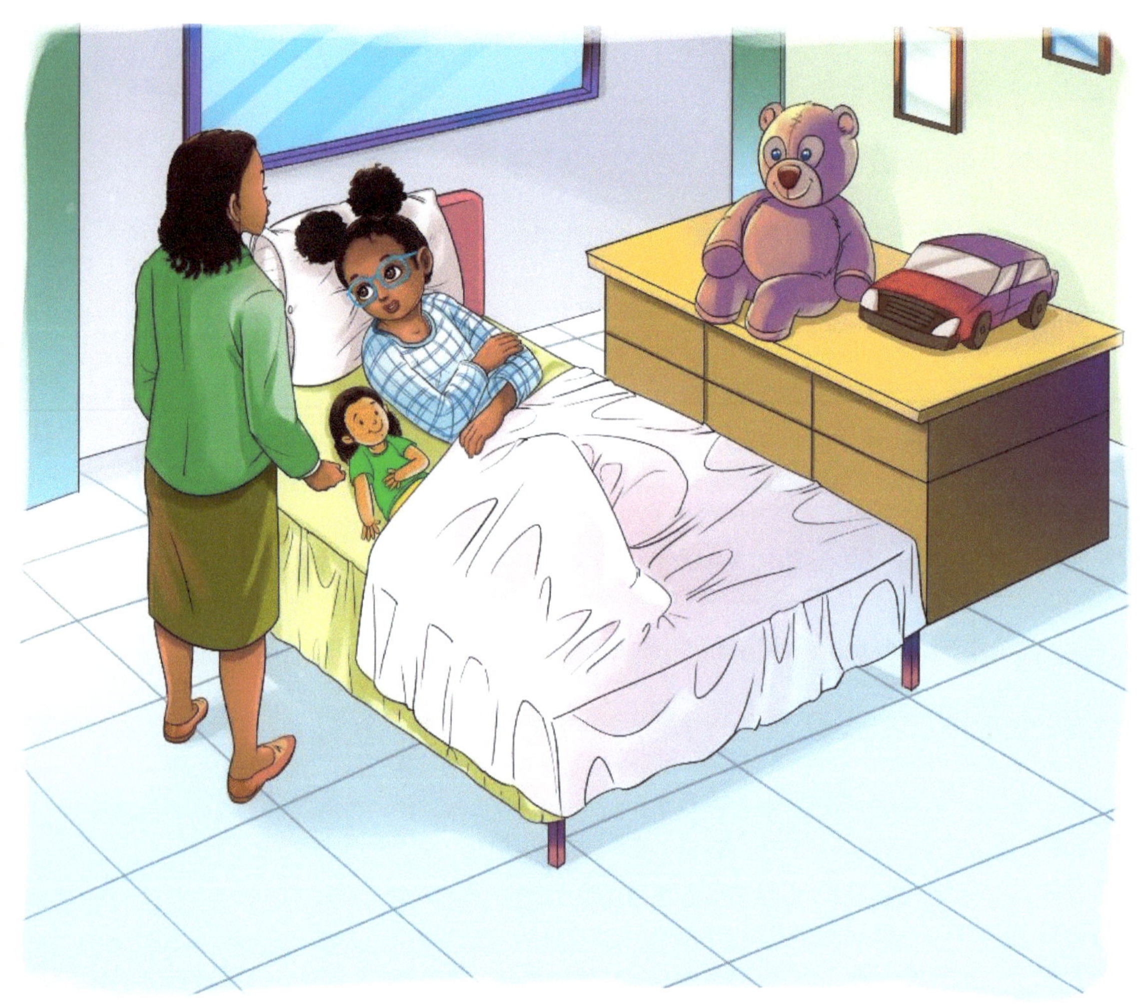

I was floating high in the sky with my best friend Shaunie. We both had on our PJ's and were laughing and playing. We then saw other kids and decided to play with them. One little girl named Sophia told us that the clouds were made of vanilla cake and marshmallows. When we got full, we drank apple juice from the invisible rain that only we could see. Then a big red hairy monster began to chase us, and we all tried to float away fast to escape it. Then Shaunie threw a huge marshmallow at it and it disappeared. We all cheered, and I woke up.

A Nurse with long hair and glasses came into my room. I didn't see her before. "Where is the other nurse?" I asked.

"She will be back in a few hours. I am Nurse Jenny and we are going to take a fun ride to the X-ray's office." I jumped up in excitement because I was tired of staying in the room. "Yep! And you get to ride in this magical wheelchair with a warm blanket too!" Nurse Jenny said, helping me get in the wheelchair. I was still in pain and began to frown.

"What's magical about it?" I asked.

"Well, every child that rides in the wheelchair, their pain will go away", Nurse Jenny said.

I was excited rolling down the hall and giggling. I felt like a princess for real at the magical castle. The X-ray table was cold and I felt the pain again. I hated that cold room and I wanted to leave. After we were all done, she gave me a lollipop for being good. I didn't want to go back to sleep, so the nurse turned on the cartoons until I fell asleep again.

The next day, I was allowed to play with some of the other kids. I played with a little girl named Lindsey who said she had cancer. We both played with some Barbie dolls. I no longer felt sad. My best friend Shaunie even visited me that evening. I didn't see her forever and I missed her a lot. We colored back in my room until it was time for her to go. I cried because I was going to miss my best friend in the whole wide world. Nurse Davenport told me that I would have to get another IV, and I just got sad and depressed. Last time, it took them about thirty minutes. So, I decided to pretend like I had to go to the bathroom because I didn't want to be stuck with any more needles.

"Patricia, I thought you had to go to the restroom?" Mommy asked.

"No, Mommy! Please don't make me go back! I don't want to be stuck again." I whined, rubbing my eyes.

"It's going to be okay. The Nurse wants to make sure you get better so they just need to get some more blood", Mommy said, giving me a big hug.

"OKKAAYYY", I whined, following Mommy back to my room.

I closed my eyes while both Mommy and Daddy held my hand. I then thought about something happy. I was with Shaunie again and we were superheroes saving other kids from the neighborhood. We flew up into the sky and chanted "Sickle Cell Sucks". That's when I opened my eyes and the IV was in. I was relieved. I didn't want to feel any more needles. I was starting to feel a little better after the doctors and nurses gave me more medicine to make my pain go away. Even through the pain, I still pushed through it. Mommy and Daddy call me "a strong Sickle Cell Warrior".

A lot of kids at my school make fun of me because my eyes are yellow. I grow sad and start to cry. Mommy and Daddy both told me that my eyes are yellow because of my Sickle Cell and it is called jaundice. Sometimes they glow in the dark. Shaunie thinks it's super cool and says I have real super powers. I try to tell the other kids, but they still make fun of me.

SICKLE
CELL
SUCKS

After staying in the hospital for five whole days, I was going home finally. I couldn't stop smiling because I was going to get to sleep in my own bed again and go back to school to see all my classmates. When I got home, Mommy and Daddy had a banner hanging up that read "Welcome Home, Patricia!" I started jumping up and down and snapping my fingers because I was excited to finally be at home.

"You are definitely our little Sickle Cell Warrior and we love you very much", Daddy said, hugging me.

"Patricia you are very special. People may not always understand, but as long as you do, that's all that matters", Mommy said.

I was happy to have a great Mommy and Daddy. I had a great time with my visit to the hospital despite my pain crisis that I was dealing with. Make sure you educate yourself on Sickle Cell Disease because it is very important!

SICKLE CELL WARRIORS

September
is
SICKLE CELL
Awareness
Month

Patricia's
Educational Workbook

Educate Yourself

and

Your Family

Sickle Cell is an inherited blood disorder

∞

Both parents must inherit the trait in order for the child to get Sickle Cell Disease

∞

SCD is not contagious; it is not like a cold or the flu which you can just catch

∞

There is no universal cure for SCD; only a bone transplant which can be really risky and can cause a lot of side effects and even death

∞

Pain is one of the main symptoms of SCD

∞

A person with SCD can live a long, quality and healthy life

∞

There is only one medicine that can reduce pain episodes with sickle cell and that is called Hydroxyurea

∞

Fatigue is another common symptom with SCD

∞

Breathing problems are common in children with SCD

∞

This disease affects many races besides African Americans

Find the Words

Sickle Cell Anemia

```
G X W M V Z F S V Z L I O B X D S
N T E A E X G T S M O T P M Y S I
I V P L L G Q S J Y H W T T U I S
N I E A D E T I R E H N I Y N C O
E L W R Q H E M O G L O B I N K N
E W F I J U W Q N Z Z J O Z V L G
R T Y A C Z B R X A J C L A P E A
C W M W F S I S I R C A C O G C I
S E T R E A T M E N T E D S H E D
R C S N O I S U F S N A R T D L I
L H U C P D Z K U U G E N E S L F
H K J P N C E L L S P E L R U T P
P P J U L D Z D C Q C I B L O O D
A I M E N A S S R S B B Y C W O H
I T R A I T X G E X W G R Y O B Z
N J Y F D F C R A F R I C A N B F
R I X B E E C K B Q O Y X B R I F
```

transfusions	treatment	hemoglobin	diagnosis
symptoms	screening	trait	malaria
African	pain	crescent	cells
blood	genes	inherited	crisis
Sickle	cell	anemia	

Let's See How Well You Know

Sickle Cell Disease

Take the short quiz.

(Circle your answers)

Sickle Cell Disease affects other races
besides African Americans.

True   or   False

In order for a child to have the full-blown disease, both parents
don't need to have the trait.

True   or   False

There is no cure for Sickle Cell Disease.

True   or   False

Pain is a common symptom of SCD.

True   or   False

SCD is contagious just like the cold and the flu.

True   or   False

Breathing problems are common with children with SCD.

True   or   False

Hydroxyurea is not the main medicine used to reduce pain
episodes.

True   or   False

Answers

1

True: Sickle Cell Disease affects people in other parts of the world, including Hispanics, and those who live in the Caribbean, India and other countries.

2

False: Both parents must inherit the trait in order for a child to get Sickle Cell Disease. If one parent has the trait and the other parent doesn't, there is a 50/50 chance that the child will be born with the disease.

3

False: Technically, there is a universal cure for SCD which is a bone marrow transplant.

4

True: Pain is definitely a common symptom. Pain varies from different parts of the body such as in the joints, arms, legs, hips, neck, back, etc. A lot of people living with SCD are constantly hospitalized due to pain crises.

5

False: A person can't catch this disease. It is genetically inherited from parents.

6

True: When the sickle cells get jammed in the arteries or vessels in the body, there isn't enough oxygen getting to the brain and other parts of the body. This can cause pain as well.

7

False: Hydroxyurea reduces pain and blood transfusions in a person living with SCD.

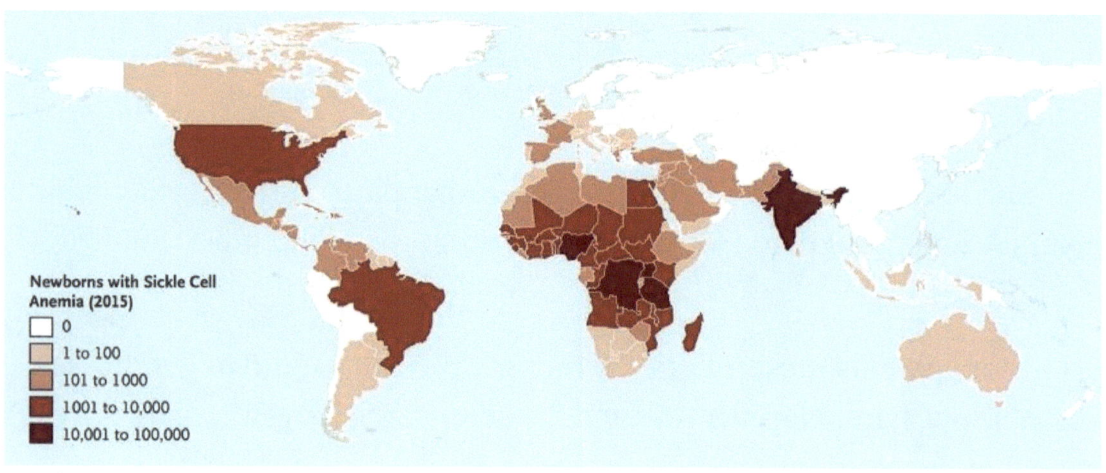

Newborns with Sickle Cell Anemia (2015)
0
1 to 100
101 to 1000
1001 to 10,000
10,001 to 100,000

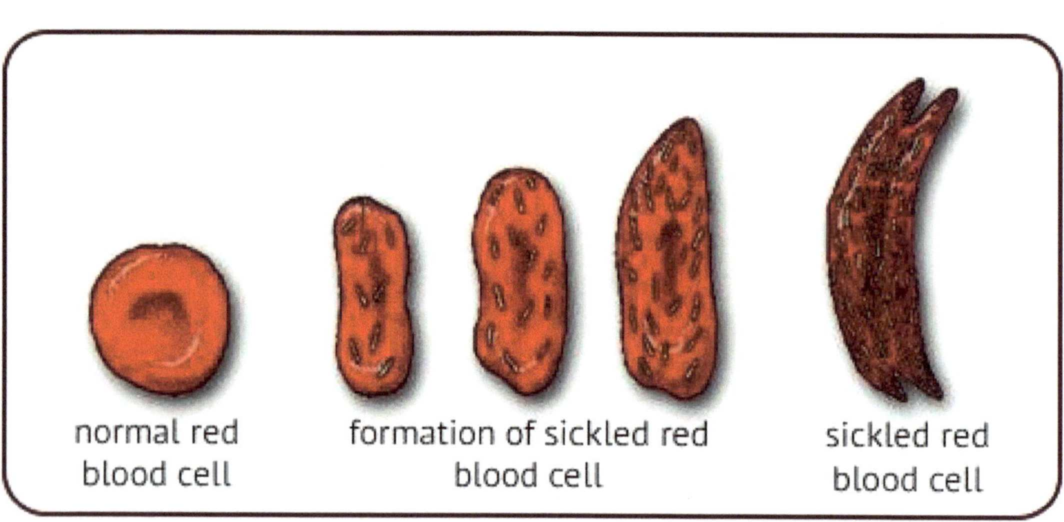

normal red
blood cell
formation of sickled red
blood cell
sickled red
blood cell

Living with
Sickle Cell

Sickle Cell Disease

Resources

To learn more about the Sickle Cell Disease, visit

www.hematology.org/Patients/Anemia/Sickle-Cell.aspx

Ways you can help out

with the Sickle Cell Disease Community

Volunteer!

Join your local SCD chapter or foundation. Visit

www.sicklecelldisease.org/support-and-community/find-member-organizations

Find your local chapter by the state you live in.

Donate!

What better way to help out with the Sickle Cell Association than to donate! There are several ways to donate to various organizations. Visit

sicklecellfoundation.org/donations

www.sicklecelldisease.org/general-donations

Become an advocate!

Even if you don't have the disease, if you know someone who suffers from it, you can become a voice in your community!

www.sicklecelldisease.org/advocacy/national-sickle-cell-advocacy-network

Epilogue

about the Author . . .

Patrice Rivers wears many hats in the world of entrepreneurship. She is currently residing in Suffolk, VA where Virginia State University's blue and orange bleed through her veins as a graduate from the HBCU in May 2009 in Petersburg, VA. She majored in Mass Communications where she had a minor in writing, earning her Bachelors of Arts degree.

Patrice started writing at the tender age of nine when creating short stories was more than just a hobby. She has a very vivid and creative imagination when it comes to words. Poetry has and will always be her first love. Since she was 15, Patrice took a strong interest in writing poems. Throughout the years, writing poetry has always been a therapeutic way for her to express her true feelings. Her creativity took her all the way to publishing her first book of poetry in 2012, entitled ***A Collection of God's Word and Motivation*** which is a great seller. In 2013, her second book of poetry, ***Lyrical Passion Tears from my Inkwell*** was published, in which she encourages and captivates her reader's attention through real situations and encouraging words. Patrice has published a total of eight books with two of them being children's books about a little girl living with the Sickle Cell Disease.

As a survivor and person living with SCD herself, the author wanted to create not only a children's book, but a series that will serve as an educational tool for kids and adults as well in communities. Patrice is also the proud owner and creator of ***That Riverz Girl Brand LLC*** which consists of different facets such as books, podcasts, interviews, magazines, literary services and its own You Tube channel.

Her magazine, ***Versafi Magazine*** is a platform for men and women of diversity who are business owners, entrepreneurs and authors. With this being her second magazine, Patrice plans to take *Versafi* to a higher level with diversity being a very important factor within her brand.

Patrice does plan to continue writing more books that relate to her life as well as children books. She is very passionate about the writing community and wants to expand her writing services to a small writing boutique, providing services to new authors, continuous authors, brands, business owners and entrepreneurs all over.

This determined boss babe is nothing more than passionate, a goal digger, creative, professional and unique with her brand. She hopes to someday expand her brand to a wider audience in the world of business.

新颖 纸 印刷 主宾国 新颖
书展 书籍
纸 书展 活力 出版 印刷 纸
文字 主宾国 文化
新颖 中国 纸 出版 新颖
文化 文化
书展 主宾国 书籍
创意
纸 书展 纸 书 籍 印刷
活力 创意 书籍 印刷
出版 主宾国 纸

about the Artist . . .

Born in 1982 in Lucknow city INDIA, Vineet Kumar Siddhartha is the leading Indian artist of the generation. He has earned a master's degree in Fine Arts in the late 2000, absorbing the acute attention to form associated with design and visualization.

Vineet Kumar Siddhartha worked in various design firms and animation studios. He has been published around the world and has won multiple awards for his work in numerous children books and comic books.

Website

saffronyellow.wordpress.com

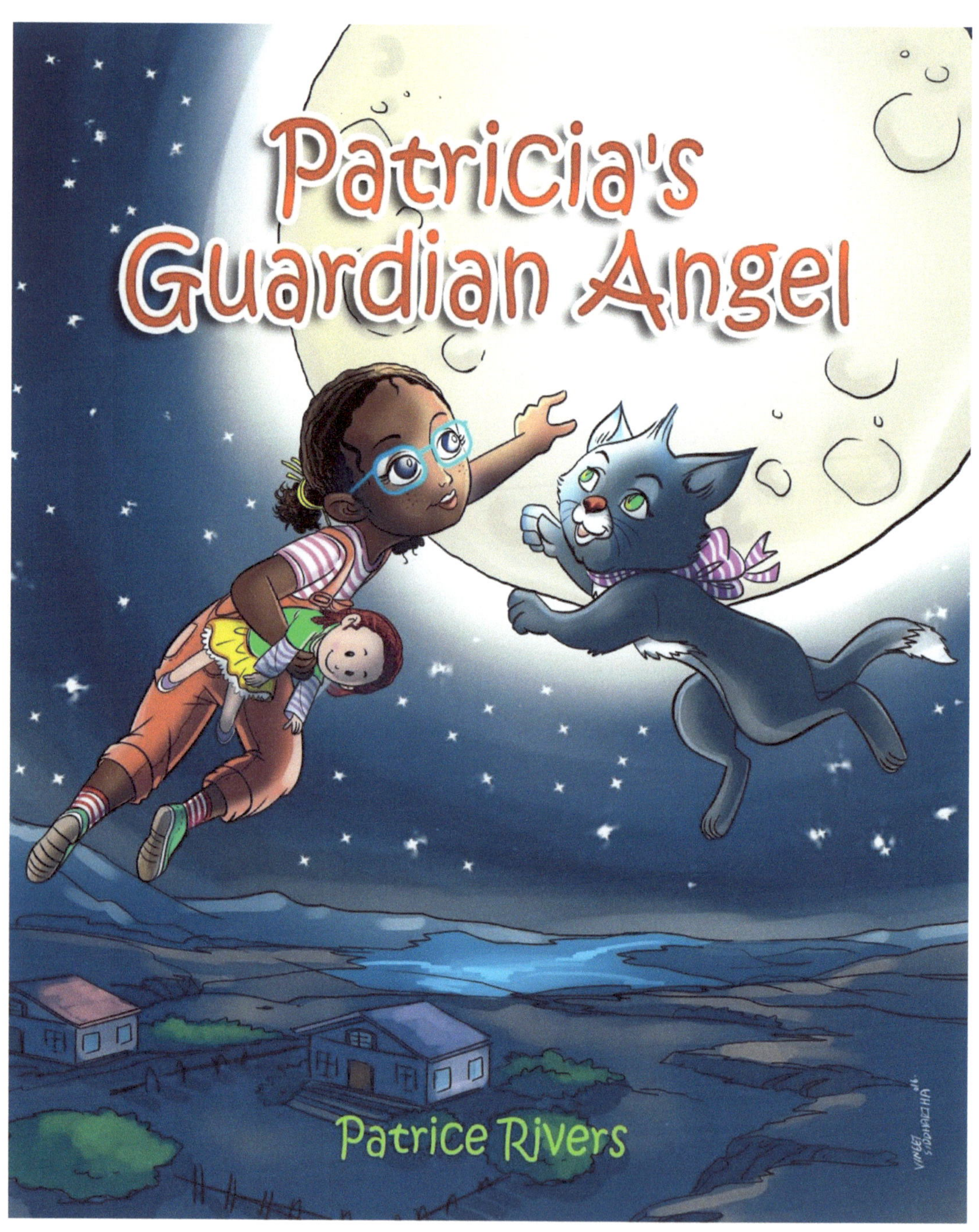

Patricia's Guardian Angel
Patrice Rivers

Lyrical Passion
Tears from my Inkwell
Patrice Nicole Rivers

For Kindle's Sake
Patrice Rivers

A Collection of God's Word and Motivation
Words of Encouragement
Patrice Rivers

A Love Scorned
A Love Scorned
Lyrical Passion
Lyrical Passion

Through My Lens
An Inspirational Book of Poetry
Patrice Rivers

Inner Child Press International

Inner Child Press International is a publishing company founded and operated by writers. Our personal publishing experiences provides us an intimate understanding of the sometimes-daunting challenges writers, new and seasoned may face in the business of publishing and marketing their creative "Written Work".

For more information:

Inner Child Press International

www.innerchildpress.com

intouch@innerchildpress.com